Step 3
Choose one, two, or three vegetables that go together

Need some ideas?

corn

squash + parsnip

Leek + cauliflower

sweet potato + carrot

Step 4
chop vegetables and add to pot

Step 5
Add water or stock to cover

Step 6
Bring to boil, then reduce to simmer

Step 7
Remove bay leaf and thyme sprigs. MASH or blend. Season.

Our Little Kitchen

Jillian Tamaki

Abrams Books for Young Readers

New York

Every Wednesday,
we come together
in this little kitchen.

Our little kitchen,
a tiny, small place,

is just big enough,
so squeeze in and make space . . .

Tie on your apron!
Roll up your sleeves!

Well,

Pans are out, oven is hot.
The kitchen's all ready,

where do we start?

See how our little garden has grown?

Remember how we pushed seeds into soil,
one by one?

What about you?

Here come the early birds,
grab your favorite seat.

The best sound in
the world is

SSSSSSLLLLLLUUUUUrRRRR

Is your body warm?

Is your belly full?

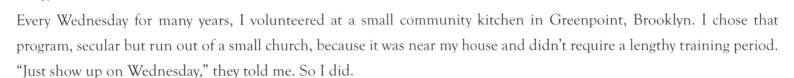

Author's Note

Every Wednesday for many years, I volunteered at a small community kitchen in Greenpoint, Brooklyn. I chose that program, secular but run out of a small church, because it was near my house and didn't require a lengthy training period. "Just show up on Wednesday," they told me. So I did.

I wasn't welcomed with open arms or even a hello. "You can start by peeling those potatoes," maybe. It was a busy, working kitchen—there was just too much to do. I put my head down, did as I was told, and tried not to get in the way. I came again the following week. And the week after that. Eventually the kitchen crew softened to me. I was part of the team.

Sometimes our kitchen had a lot: in the full burst of summer when we harvested from the garden, upstate farms donated produce, or we had just held a fundraiser. But often we had much less to work with. Many meals in the colder months were cobbled together with not-ideal ingredients, less beautiful and more functional—but always a full meal, nourishing and on time(ish). There was no other option.

The neighborhood in which we worked was changing. Rents were on the rise. The economy crashed. When things are stretched thin, food is often the first thing to be cut. As passionate and tenacious as we were, our little kitchen was not a solution to our problems of food, housing, and economic insecurity—it merely provided one meal on Wednesday nights.

Still, we kept showing up. We activated our spirits, used our hands. Nourished our bodies so that we might shout NO to injustice, and stood arm in arm as we faced down our different struggles. We are often told that a single person can change the world. Just think about what many of us can accomplish—with our bodies, voices, votes, and hearts—together.

Thank you

Ann C, Emily, and the Greenpoint kitchen crew. Joshna, Jo,
The Stop Community Food Centre, and Parkdale Project Read.

Lis, Steven, Jael, Eleanor, Jon, Zainab, Michael, ST.

Emma, Pamela, Alison, Tamar, and the myriad people who help
bring books into the world at Abrams. Semareh and the team
at Groundwood Books.

This book is dedicated to Christine Z.

The illustrations in this book were done with a nib and ink. The colors were made on the computer.

A portion of Abrams's profits from the sale of this book will be donated to the Greenpoint Hunger Program.
For more information, visit abramsbooks.com/OurLittleKitchen.

Cataloging-in-Publication Data has been applied for and may be obtained from the Library of Congress.

ISBN 978-1-4197-4655-0

Text and illustrations copyright © 2020 Jillian Tamaki

Book design by Pamela Notarantonio

Printed and bound in U.S.A.

10 9 8 7 6 5 4 3 2

Abrams Books for Young Readers are available at special discounts when purchased in quantity for
premiums and promotions as well as fundraising or educational use. Special editions can also be created
to specification. For details, contact specialsales@abramsbooks.com or the address below.

Abrams® is a registered trademark of Harry N. Abrams, Inc.

ABRAMS The Art of Books
195 Broadway, New York, NY 10007
abramsbooks.com

FSC
www.fsc.org
MIX
Paper from
responsible sources
FSC™ C002589

About the Author

Jillian Tamaki is an illustrator, comics artist, and teacher living in Toronto, Ontario. She is the cocreator, with her cousin Mariko Tamaki, of the graphic novels *Skim* and *This One Summer*, the latter of which won a Caldecott Honor. *Our Little Kitchen* is the second picture book she both wrote and illustrated. Her first, *They Say Blue*, an exploration of our perception and experience of the natural world, was released in 2018. She is OK at cooking, but very good at chopping and peeling. Visit her online at jilliantamaki.com.

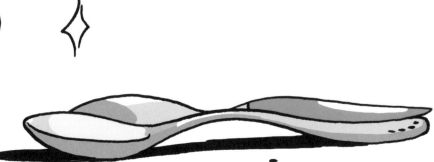